W9-CMI-800

Dear Parent:

Congratulations! Your child is taking the first steps on an exciting journey. The destination? Independent reading!

STEP INTO READING® will help your child get there. The program offers five steps to reading success. Each step includes fun stories and colorful art. There are also Step into Reading Sticker Books, Step into Reading Math Readers, Step into Reading Write-In Readers, Step into Reading Phonics Readers, and Step into Reading Phonics First Steps! Boxed Sets—a complete literacy program with something for every child.

Learning to Read, Step by Step!

Ready to Read **Preschool–Kindergarten**
• big type and easy words • rhyme and rhythm • picture clues
For children who know the alphabet and are eager to begin reading.

Reading with Help **Preschool–Grade 1**
• basic vocabulary • short sentences • simple stories
For children who recognize familiar words and sound out new words with help.

Reading on Your Own **Grades 1–3**
• engaging characters • easy-to-follow plots • popular topics
For children who are ready to read on their own.

Reading Paragraphs **Grades 2–3**
• challenging vocabulary • short paragraphs • exciting stories
For newly independent readers who read simple sentences with confidence.

Ready for Chapters **Grades 2–4**
• chapters • longer paragraphs • full-color art
For children who want to take the plunge into chapter books but still like colorful pictures.

STEP INTO READING® is designed to give every child a successful reading experience. The grade levels are only guides. Children can progress through the steps at their own speed, developing confidence in their reading, no matter what their grade.

Remember, a lifetime love of reading starts with a single step!

For my nieces and nephews,
Mark, Abigail, Jessica, Raina, and Ryan
—D.W.L.

For Jeff and Wes,
thanks for the inspiration!
—Jenny

 Published in the United States by Random House Children's Books, a division of Random House, Inc., New York, and simultaneously in Canada by Random House of Canada Limited, Toronto.

www.stepintoreading.com

Educators and librarians, for a variety of teaching tools, visit us at
www.randomhouse.com/teachers

Library of Congress Cataloging-in-Publication Data
Landolf, Diane Wright.
Hog and Dog / by Diane Wright Landolf ; illustrated by Jenny B Harris.
p. cm. — (Step into reading. Step 1)
SUMMARY: Two friends learn that, while each of them is good at some games and bad at others, they can still have fun together.
ISBN 0-375-83165-7 (trade) — ISBN 0-375-93165-1 (lib. bdg.)
[1. Play—Fiction. 2. Friendship—Fiction. 3. Dogs—Fiction. 4. Pigs—Fiction.] I. Harris, Jenny B, [Date] ill. II. Title. III. Series: Step into reading. Step 1 book.
PZ7.L2317345Ho 2005 [E]—dc22 2004020521

Printed in the United States of America First Edition 10 9 8 7 6 5 4 3 2 1

STEP INTO READING®

Hog and Dog

by Diane Wright Landolf
illustrated by Jenny B Harris

Random House New York

Ball hog.

Tall dog.

Leap frog.

Oh, no!

Not Hog!

Swim race.

Splash! Splash!

Fish is first.

Dog is last.

Hog and Dog
play tag.

Hog zigs.

Dog zags.

Hide-and-seek.

Hog sees Dog peek!

Dog is sad.

Now Hog feels bad.

But wait!

Ding-dong!

"Ping-Pong?"

Hog and Dog.

Friends till the end!